Photo by Sally Deems

Dedicated to

the Monarch Butterfly

Pretty Betty Butterfly

Betty is a butterfly

who lives in a garden
filled with friends.

There are toads

and chipmunks,

bugs and birds.

The fun just never ends!

Betty spends her summer days

flitting from flower

to flower,

sipping nectar
from the blossoms,

hour after sun-filled hour.

Sunshine helps
the plants to grow
and warms Betty's
pretty wings.

every afternoon

she meets her friends,

and they do

such wonderful things...

Beulah Bee

and

Herbie Hummingbird,

and a merry moth
named Morrie.

The plants
all love it
when they
come.

They share a happy story!

So if you're near a garden,

and something fluttery

catches your eye,

you'd better take a closer look...

...it might be Betty saying "Hi!"

Author:
Sally Deems

Sally has been writing professionally for over 20 years.
Her work has won recognition through the National Calendar Awards
as well as the Louie Awards, which honor originality and creativity
in the greeting card industry. Sally is passionate about the natural
world and is helping others make a personal connection
with nature through her writing.
She lives in NE Ohio on the shore of Lake Erie
where she tends several flower gardens filled
with butterflies and other friends.

Illustrator:
Wendy Fedan

Wendy is a professional illustrator/designer in Cleveland, Ohio.
She graduated from the Cleveland Institute of Art in 1996 with a BFA
in Illustration and a Minor in Creative Writing.
Wendy runs a website and blog called Create-A-Way
(www.createawaytoday.com) to promote positive, creative
and spiritual living. She also loves to visit schools, speaking with kids
to promote creative expression through writing and journaling.

For more FUN
with Betty Butterfly
& Friends

visit her website:

www.prettybettybutterfly.com

Made in the USA
San Bernardino, CA
29 April 2014